To my family and cats,
including Lucky Bumper, who recently
passed away after 18 joyful years.

www.mascotbooks.com

JOY

©2019 Audrey Kai Yoon. All Rights Reserved. No part of this publication may be reproduced, stored in a retrieval system or transmitted in any form by any means electronic, mechanical, or photocopying, recording or otherwise without the permission of the author.

For more information, please contact:
Mascot Books
620 Herndon Parkway, Suite 320
Herndon, VA 20170
info@mascotbooks.com

Library of Congress Control Number: 2019900364

CPSIA Code: PRT0319A
ISBN-13: 978-1-64307-225-8

Printed in the United States

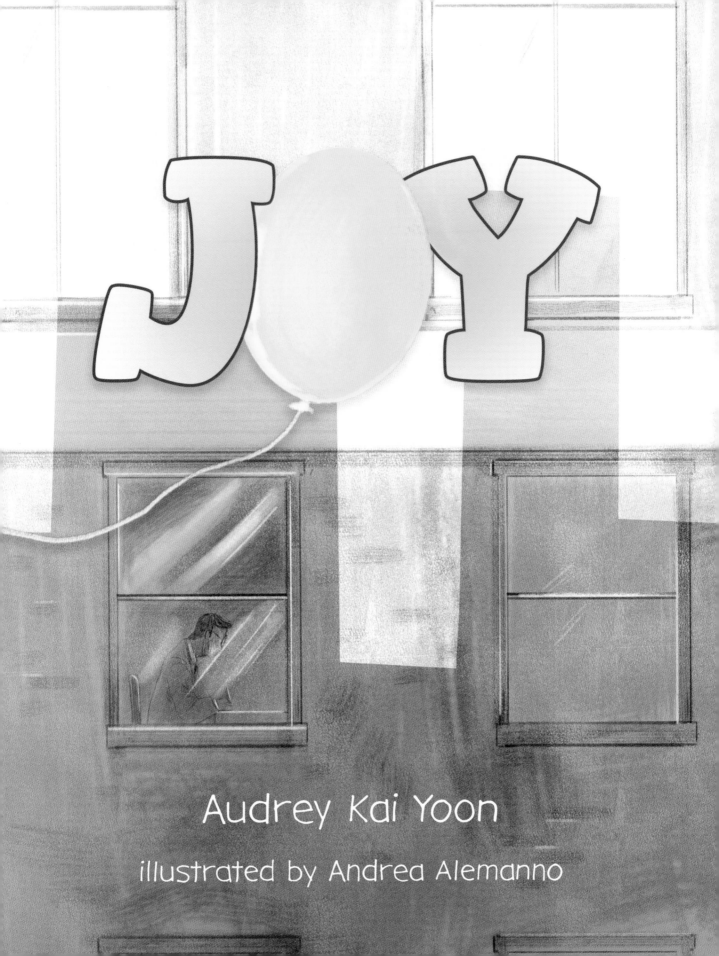

JOY

Audrey Kai Yoon

illustrated by Andrea Alemanno

One fateful day, a yellow balloon was released into the sky. Although it was just a balloon, it was brimming with joy.

The balloon watched a man who was as dull as the money he lived for. He was in desperate need of joy.

The man didn't notice the balloon. But the balloon noticed the disheartened man.

The balloon pursued the man endlessly,
day after day.

At last, the man started to notice the strange yellow balloon that always seemed to be by him. Finally, the man turned to the balloon, curiosity and suspicion shining in his eyes. The balloon turned and started to float down the road. Still suspicious, the man followed.

The balloon led the man out of the
city and through the countryside.

They crossed a river and
went through a forest.

Away from the dreary city, the man began to feel something he hadn't felt in a long time. A bubbling, happy feeling. Memories of hiking up a mountain with his parents while they were still alive returned to him.

But then he also remembered how his parents hadn't made enough money to feed him. And how he had sworn that he would make enough money so that his family would never go hungry.

The man ran away from the yellow balloon and back to the city as fast as he could. He ran to his money, to what he thought made him happy. He worked harder than ever before. He rarely slept. He rarely ate.

He worked unneeded hours just to fill his hunger for money. Joy never came to him as he worked. He didn't see the yellow balloon again.

Then one day, his wife came to visit him
at the office. She called their family
nothing but a name. She told him that his
children missed their father and
were beginning to forget him.
Realizing what he had
done to himself, and
his family, the
man wept.

The next morning, the man was surprised to see the yellow balloon outside his window. He felt a small flutter of joy in his chest. This time, he willingly followed the balloon out of the city and away from his money, the money that had brought him nothing.

The balloon led him through the countryside again, but this time his family was there waiting for him. With tears in his eyes, the man hugged his children and wife. He now knew that money would never give him true joy. He needed something that brings joy like no other.

FAMILY.

ABOUT THE AUTHOR

Audrey Yoon lives in the suburbs of Chicago with her mom; dad; older sister, Miya; and younger brother, Luke.

She enjoys playing with her family's two cats, Elastigirl and Mr. Incredible, who are themselves siblings. Audrey also likes to bake cookies, cakes, brownies, and pies. She misses her cat, Lucky Bumper, who brought her family much joy.

Audrey wrote this story for her 6th grade English class when she was 11 years old. The assignment was to write a children's book. She was inspired by a short film about a paper airplane she saw at summer camp, Chi-KO. This is where the idea and image of the yellow balloon emerged.

When asked if the story is about her dad, Audrey says no. It's not about any one person. The story is about finding balance and paying attention to the opportunities for joy, opportunities that float right by us all the time.

MASCOT®
BOOKS

Have a book idea?
Contact us at:

info@mascotbooks.com | www.mascotbooks.com